To my little princesses
Beatrice, Carolina, Carlotta, and Sofia
and my little princes
Andrea-Beni and Edoardo

Atheneum Books for Young Readers
An imprint of Simon & Schuster Children's Publishing Division
1230 Avenue of the Americas
New York, New York 10020

The text of this book was set in Akzidenz Grotesk.
The illustrations were rendered in cut paper collage.

Printed in Hong Kong
2 4 6 8 10 9 7 5 3 1

Library of Congress Cataloging-in-Publication Data
Montresor, Beni.
Hansel and Gretel / Beni Montresor.—1st ed.
p.   cm.
Summary: A retelling of the well-known tale in which two children are lost in the woods
and find their way home despite an encounter with a wicked witch.
ISBN 0-689-84144-2
[1. Fairy tales. 2. Folklore—Germany.] I. Hansel and Gretel. English. II. Title.
PZ8.M78 Han 2001
398.2'0943'02—dc21
[E]   00-040142

FIRST
EDITION

HaNSeL and GReTeL

BENI MONTRESOR

ATHENEUM BOOKS FOR YOUNG READERS
New York   London   Toronto   Sydney   Singapore

Hansel and Gretel lived
in a very poor home. . . .

One day, when there was nothing more to eat, their mother sent them into the woods to look for strawberries.

That evening, by the time their father came home, the children had not returned from the woods. He and their mother began to worry.

They knew that in the woods there was sometimes an evil monster, not to mention terrifying devils and witches. One of these witches, more wicked than others, eats children.

In the woods Hansel and Gretel picked many strawberries, but because they were so hungry, they ate them all right away and then fell asleep.

They dreamed that beautiful angels came down from heaven to watch over them and protect them from monsters and witches.

The next morning, when they awakened, they discovered that the woods had vanished and in its place stood a wonderful castle. From the castle drifted the aroma of magnificent foods being prepared. Hungry again, they entered . . .

. . . and they were immediately
taken prisoner by the witch who
eats children.

The witch locked all the doors, and put Hansel in a cage. She forced Gretel to light a fire to cook him. Hansel and Gretel could hear the murmurs of other children hidden away in the castle. Gretel knew she must do something.

When the witch turned her back just once, Gretel seized the witch's magic wand and set her brother free.

Hansel and Gretel gave the evil witch a shove. Kicking and screaming, she tumbled into the fire and burned up.

Then Hansel and Gretel freed all the children held prisoner by the witch, who celebrated them as heroes, and everything ended joyfully for everyone.